91

J
B
HENRY

Fisher, Leonard
Everett.

Prince Henry the
Navigator.

$14.95

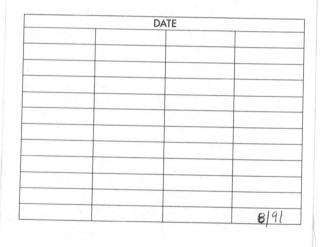

DATE			
			8/91

PRINCE HENRY THE NAVIGATOR

PRINCE HENRY THE NAVIGATOR

LEONARD EVERETT FISHER

Macmillan Publishing Company   New York

Collier Macmillan Publishers   London

CHRONOLOGY OF THE IBERIAN PENINSULA, 711–1498

711. . . . . . . The Moors invade the Iberian Peninsula.

1249. . . . . . . The Moors are driven out of Portugal.

1385. . . . . . . John I becomes king of Portugal.

1394. . . . . . . Prince Henry is born.

1415. . . . . . . The Portuguese capture Ceuta, Morocco.

1416. . . . . . . Prince Henry opens his school of navigation.

1420. . . . . . . Madeira is discovered.

1427. . . . . . . The Azores are discovered.

1434. . . . . . . The Portuguese sail past Cape Bojador.

1444. . . . . . . The West African slave trade begins.

1451. . . . . . . Christopher Columbus is born.

1460. . . . . . . Prince Henry dies.

1476. . . . . . . Columbus is shipwrecked near Sagres.

1481. . . . . . . John II becomes king of Portugal.

1482. . . . . . . A Portuguese ship reaches the Congo River.

1484. . . . . . . King John II rejects Columbus's sailing plans.
Columbus presents himself to the Spanish monarchs.

1488. . . . . . . Bartolomeu Dias sails around the Cape of Good Hope.

1492. . . . . . . Ferdinand and Isabella approve Columbus's plans.
Columbus reaches North America.

1498. . . . . . . Vasco da Gama reaches India.

To William B. R. Reiss

With appreciation to Dr. Jacob Smit,
Professor of History, Columbia University

10   9   8   7   6   5   4   3   2   1

The text of this book is set in 14 point Galliard.
The black-and-white paintings were rendered in acrylic paints on paper.

Library of Congress Cataloging-in-Publication Data
Fisher, Leonard Everett. Prince Henry the Navigator/ Leonard Everett Fisher. — 1st ed.   p.   cm. Summary: A biography of that Portuguese prince whose vision and whose school of navigation significantly affected all later explorers who charted the unknown.
1. Henry, Infante of Portugal, 1394–1460 — Juvenile literature. 2. Explorers — Portugal — Biography — Juvenile literature. [1. Henry the Navigator, 1394–1460. 2. Explorers.] I. Title.
G286.H5F57   1990   910.92 — dc20   [B]   [92]
89-28068 CIP   AC   ISBN 0-02-735231-5

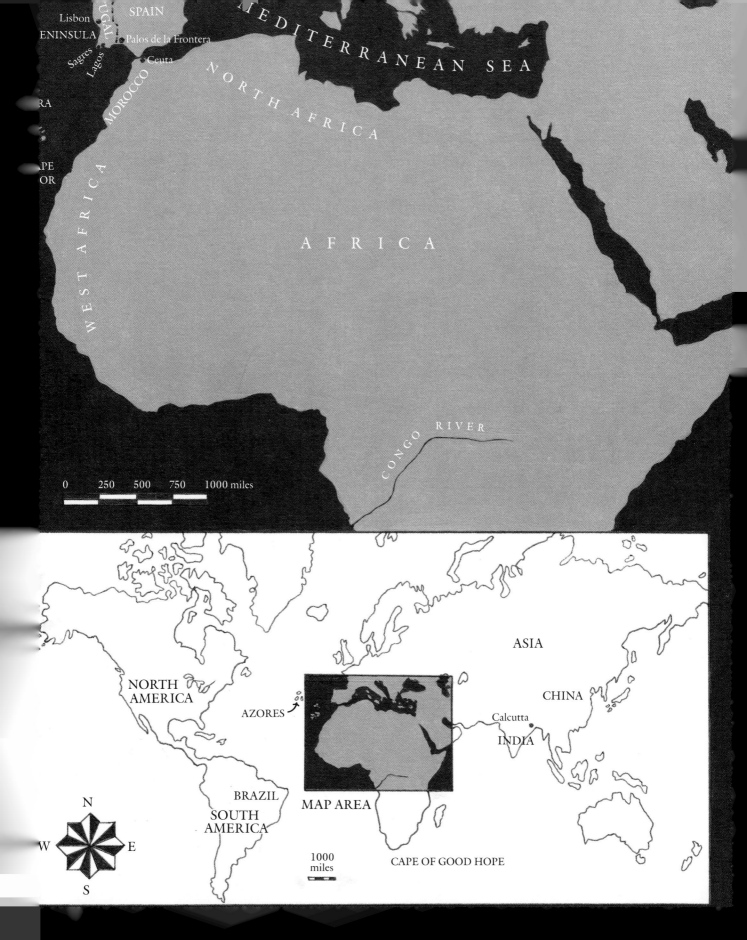

Between 711 and 1249, North African Moslems — Moors — ruled Portugal and Spain. Made up of loosely knit kingdoms, the two countries shared the Iberian Peninsula on Christian Europe's southwest corner. Islam, the Moslem religion, nearly replaced Christianity on the entire peninsula.

Beginning in 1064, Christian armies made up of French, Spanish, and Portuguese knights began to push the Moors south and finally drove them from Portugal in 1249. For the next 166 years, the Moors attacked Portuguese ships from Ceuta, Morocco, their North African stronghold.

Portugal's King John I was determined to end Moorish sea power. On July 25, 1415, he left Lisbon with two hundred warships. With him were his three sons, Peter, Ferdinand, and twenty-one-year-old Prince Henry.

The appearance of the armada off Ceuta caught the Moors by surprise. The young princes stormed ashore with their troops. Ceuta fell on August 24, 1415. A great victory celebration was held in Lisbon, where Henry and his brothers were knighted for their bravery.

Now Portugal controlled the shipping lanes in and out of the Mediterranean Sea. African gold, jewels, and grain, and Indian spices and rare woods poured into Portuguese markets. Portugal's conquest of Ceuta made her a rich and powerful maritime nation. But if Portugal was to remain rich and powerful, she had to explore more of Africa and to reach India.

Peter and Ferdinand longed for more victories, but Prince Henry had other goals. He wanted a fast, practical route to the riches of India. And he wanted to find out more about the world, of which so little was known in 1415.

Henry wanted to find Prester John, too. Ever since he was a small boy, he had heard stories of Prester John, a white Christian king who some thought ruled a huge treasure-laden empire in either Africa or Asia. But no one could confirm the existence of such a person or empire. Henry had to find out if Prester John was real. If he was, Henry would make an alliance with him, joining Portugal to what might be the richest land on earth.

Henry knew that India and China were located to the east, but he did not know how to reach these countries by sea. There were no accurate maps to point sailors in the right direction. If Prester John could be found, he would provide some answers. But finding him was another problem.

Long-distance sea routes had not yet been established. Sailors did not voyage to far-off places. Most captains sailed close to land and usually in daylight. The Portuguese had heard of Madeira, a nearby group of islands, but they did not know exactly where it lay.

Prince Henry vowed to find a way to sail into distant, unknown waters, seek out what was there, and return—even if it took him his whole life.

To prepare for his expeditions, the young prince went to Cape Saint Vincent, Portugal's — and Europe's — most southwesterly point. There, at Sagres, miles from Lisbon and civilization, he built a house and chapel high above the crashing sea. On that hot, lonely, windswept cliff, he pondered the mystery of what lay beyond the horizon.

Henry amassed a library of books and maps. He brought ship captains, navigators, mapmakers, astronomers, and geographers to Sagres and formed a school of navigation.

Henry thought that only Africa to the south stood between himself and India. But no one knew the size and shape of Africa, since European ships had never sailed beyond Cape Bojador, on Africa's Atlantic bulge. Sailors did not dare attempt such a trip, some because they believed that if northern waters froze, southern waters boiled. No sailor wanted to be boiled alive! Other sailors still believed the earth was flat and that ships would fall off any of its watery sides. That notion had long since been proven ridiculous by ship captains, astronomers, and geographers. Henry brushed aside all such nonsense and continued to plan his expeditions.

He prayed in his chapel for guidance, studied in the quiet of his library, and stood for hours at the edge of the cliff, watching the ocean. Finally he reasoned that one had to sail south along the African coast and eventually turn east to reach India. Henry offered prize money to anyone who would challenge the sea and find India.

Henry prepared carefully for his expeditions. His scholars improved three tools that mariners used to find their way: the circular astrolabe, the triangular quadrant, and the compass. The astrolabe measured the angle of stars above the horizon. The quadrant measured the height of the sun or stars above the horizon. Both devices helped to find latitude, one's position north or south of the equator, the horizontal imaginary line that circles the earth at the same distance from the North and South poles. Sailors still did not know how to plot longitude, one's position east or west of the imaginary line that circles the earth vertically through the North and South poles.

The third tool, the compass, was used to set a course in any direction — north, south, east, or west. Henry had a huge compass face built into the paving stones of his courtyard to train his captains. These few improvements enabled mariners to navigate out of sight of land without the fear of becoming lost.

Next Henry sent his heavy ships on trial runs along the North African coast. The captains made maps and charted currents, winds, and depths. Henry was too busy to go on any of these voyages, but he wanted to know what had occurred every minute during the expeditions. He ordered his captains to keep daily written records, or logs, of their activities and course at sea. No one had ever done that before. Captains who did not return with such records were dismissed.

In 1420 Prince Henry's ships finally found Madeira. The group of islands rose out of the Atlantic Ocean four hundred miles off the northwest African coast. It lay farther west than any European ship had sailed since the Vikings had voyaged to North America five hundred years earlier—and since the Romans had seen Madeira about sixteen hundred years before.

The school of navigation grew with the promise of great discoveries. Prince Henry, still too busy to sail on any of his expeditions, became impatient with the progress of his ships. He was unhappy with the plodding, clumsy vessels. He wanted a faster, wider, longer ship, one that could catch the slightest breeze or cut through the heaviest seas; a ship with a shallow draft and a rudder that would turn her quickly. Henry's shipbuilders in neighboring Lagos gave him what he wanted—a new type of vessel, the caravel.

Now Henry was ready for more ambitious expeditions. He sent his caravels far out into the Atlantic Ocean. In 1427 his captains discovered the Azores, a group of islands one thousand miles west of Sagres. And on Azore beaches they found strange wood carvings, plants, dead animals and people, all washed ashore by strong ocean currents. The sightings convinced Henry's captains that India must be only a short distance to the west.

Henry was stubborn. He persisted in his plan to find India by going around Africa. His caravels edged farther south. His captains brought home gold to finance more voyages and established trading towns on the African coast.

In 1434 Henry's caravels sailed around Cape Bojador. In 1444, not content with trading goods for gold, his captains began kidnapping black West Africans and selling them in Lagos as slaves. Henry did nothing to stop the practice. He needed slavery to finance the costly expeditions. Later he ordered his men to halt these kidnappings, but several unsavory captains continued to widen the slave trade. Within two hundred years, it would spill onto the American continent, whose existence was unknown to Prince Henry and his captains.

By 1460 Henry had run out of money and could no longer finance his expeditions. He died that year at Sagres.

Portuguese captains continued to hold Prince Henry's vision. In 1482 a Portuguese ship sailed to the mouth of the Congo River. Six years later, Bartolomeu Dias sailed around the Cape of Good Hope. Henry's dream of reaching India by sailing south around Africa was fulfilled on May 20, 1498, when Vasco da Gama arrived with a fleet of four ships at Calcutta. Only Henry's longing to find Prester John remained unsatisfied. No one ever discovered proof of him or his empire.

Prince Henry's school of navigation was the first maritime institute in the world for deepwater research. There information was gathered and studied, and expeditions were sent out to chart the unknown. While Henry himself never sailed on his ships, he is called Henry the Navigator because he made it possible for sailors to find their way at sea with greater accuracy. Prince Henry expanded the oceanic frontier, leading to the discovery of the Americas.

MORE ABOUT HENRY THE NAVIGATOR

Sixteen years after Henry's death, a merchant ship from Genoa, Italy, was sunk near Sagres by a Portuguese-French fleet. Twenty-five-year-old Christopher Columbus, a crewman, survived and was washed ashore. He made his way to Lisbon, where one of his brothers sold mariners' supplies.

Columbus caught Portugal's "sea fever" and became a ship captain. He believed that Prince Henry had sent his ships to India in the wrong direction—south and east instead of west! He failed to convince Portugal's King John II to send him due west to India. That year, 1484, he took his plans to the Spanish monarchs, Ferdinand and Isabella. They approved the voyage eight years later. On August 3, 1492, Columbus and his three ships, the Niña, the Pinta, and the Santa Maria, slipped out of Palos de la Frontera, Spain. Two months later they discovered a hemisphere.

Columbus's ships were caravels. They were designed at Prince Henry's school of navigation. Columbus found his way across the Atlantic Ocean by using the compass, which was improved at Prince Henry's school. He rarely used the quadrant and never used the astrolabe. But, thanks to Prince Henry, Columbus kept ships' logs, now a standard practice at sea.

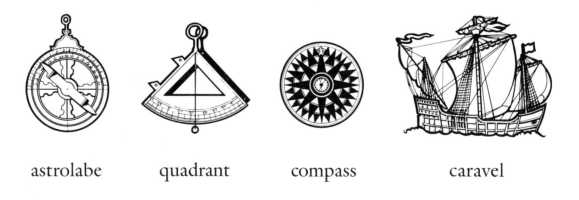

astrolabe   quadrant   compass   caravel